Necker Island

French Frigate Shoals

Nihoa Island

Kaua'i

Ni'ihau

O'ahu

Moloka'i

Lana'i

Maui

Kaho'olawe

Hawai'i

O C E A N

N
W E
S

DISCOVER HAWAI'I'S MARINE MAMMALS
Written and Illustrated by Katherine Orr

Published and distributed by

ISLAND HERITAGE
P U B L I S H I N G
A DIVISION OF THE MADDEN CORPORATION

Cover and book design by Jui-Lien L. Fletcher
Second edition, Second printing 1995

Please address orders and correspondence to:

ISLAND HERITAGE
99-880 Iwaena Street
Aiea, Hawaii 96701
(808) 487-7299

Printed in Hong Kong

DISCOVER
HAWAI'I'S
Marine Mammals

Written and Illustrated by Katherine Orr

Contents

Early morning sun warms the March air as a monk seal hauls itself from the surf onto the cool sand of a Hawaiian beach. It has spent the night hunting for food. Now it is looking for a quiet beach to sleep on while it digests its meal. Outside the reef, a group of dolphins swims slowly along the coast. A seabird swoops low over them, looks for fish, then flies away. Suddenly, a huge, black shape erupts from the deep sea beyond the dolphins and falls back again in a giant splash of foam. A moment later, it rolls along the surface and blows a plume of mist into the air. It is a humpback whale, one of the largest animals on earth, and it has come to Hawai'i's waters to breed.

Seals, whales, and dolphins are all marine mammals—mammals that live in the sea. As mammals, they breathe air through lungs and drink their mothers' milk after they are born. They are also able to maintain a warm body temperature even in very cold oceans and they have hair. Yes, even whales and dolphins have a few hairs at some time in their lives.

WHALES AND DOLPHINS— DESIGNED FOR LIFE AT SEA

Unlike seals, whales and dolphins never come ashore. Their bodies are designed for life in water. They cannot crawl with their flippers or tails, and their streamlined shapes—round and narrower at both ends—are designed to move through water easily and quickly. Their nose openings, or **blowholes**, are placed on top of their heads so they can breathe while swimming at all times. Whales seem to sleep in short naps, resting near the surface with their eyes closed and taking a breath of air every ten or fifteen minutes.

Scientists place whales in two groups: those with teeth and those without. Dolphins and porpoises belong to the group of whales with teeth called **toothed whales**. Their cone-shaped teeth are designed to grab

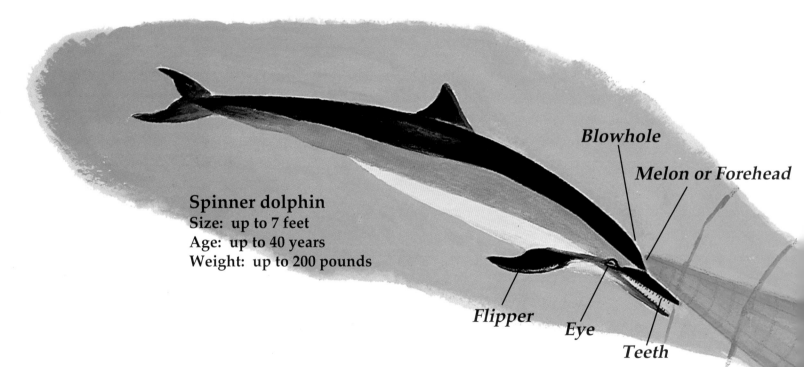

Spinner dolphin
Size: up to 7 feet
Age: up to 40 years
Weight: up to 200 pounds

Blowhole

Melon or Forehead

Flipper

Eye

Teeth

at the surface. The blowhole stays closed when the whale is underwater.

Whales and dolphins breathe at will—not steadily and automatically as we do. This means they cannot breathe while they sleep. Scientists think dolphins manage to sleep by keeping one half of their brain awake large fish and squid. Humpback whales belong to the group called **baleen whales**. **Baleen** (be-LEEN) is a strip of horny material that grows down from the whale's upper jaw in a stiff curtain. The inside edge of each strip is shredded like a frayed rope. Together, the strips of baleen form a strainer

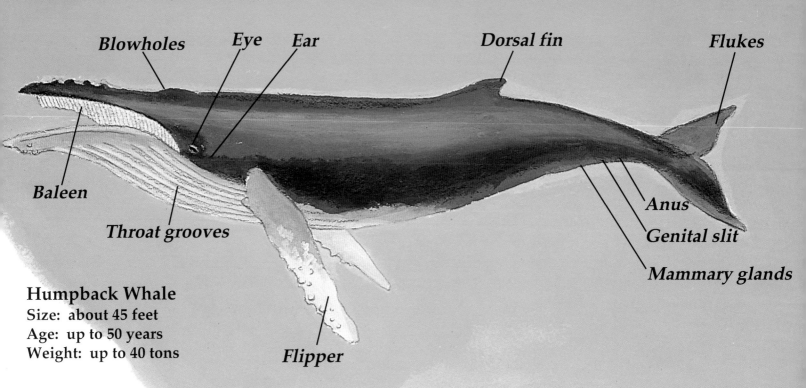

Blowholes   Eye   Ear   Dorsal fin   Flukes

Baleen

Throat grooves

Anus

Genital slit

Mammary glands

Humpback Whale
Size: about 45 feet
Age: up to 50 years
Weight: up to 40 tons

Flipper

that sieves small animals out of the water. A feeding whale takes in a mouthful of sea water full of small bits of food, then pushes the water out through the baleen. The food stays trapped inside the mouth where it can be swallowed. Folds in the skin along the whale's underside allow the mouth and throat to expand like a balloon so the whale can take in huge mouthfuls of sea water.

Dolphins and other toothed whales have a special hearing sense called **echolocation** (eh-ko-lo-KAY-shun), or **sonar** (SO-nar). They make very high sounds that travel out from their heads and bounce off objects around them. By comparing the sounds they send out to the sounds that return, they can examine their surroundings and find food. Using echolocation, dolphins can even examine the insides of animals.

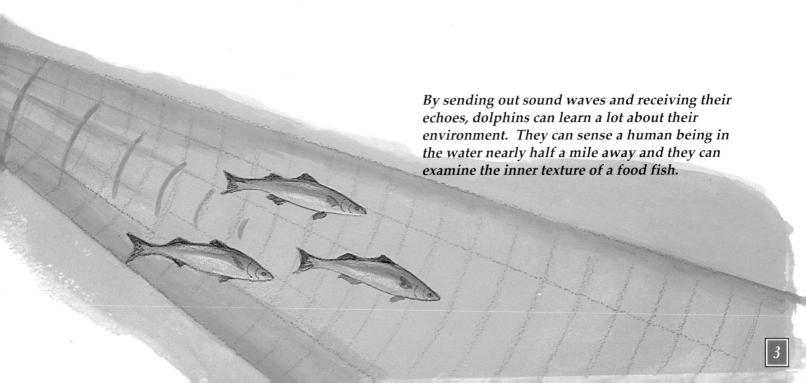

By sending out sound waves and receiving their echoes, dolphins can learn a lot about their environment. They can sense a human being in the water nearly half a mile away and they can examine the inner texture of a food fish.

HAWAI'I'S HUMPBACK WHALES

Migration

Humpback whales come to Hawai'i each year to mate and give birth. They arrive in a stream of ones, twos and threes throughout the winter. Someone usually sees the first whale of the season in November, but most humpbacks start appearing in January. Young whales and pregnant females are the first to arrive. Adult males and adult females that are not pregnant arrive next. By mid-February to mid-March, the number of whales in Hawai'i reaches its peak—about 2,000, say some scientists. But all the whales are never here at one time.

Even before some whales arrive, other whales are heading north to Alaska again. Females with their new **calves** are the last to leave. Usually, they are all gone by the end of May. They return to the cold waters off Alaska to spend the summer feeding. For six months, Hawai'i will have no humpback whales in its waters and then they will return.

To get from Alaska to Hawai'i, the whales must swim 2,000 to 3,000 miles each way across open ocean. They probably use water temperature and ocean currents to

help guide them, but they may be able to sense direction as well. Their brains contain **magnetite** (MAG-ne-tite), a magnetic material found in the brains of some birds, whales and fish. Scientists think magnetite acts like a built-in compass that helps these animals sense changes in the earth's magnetic field.

Feeding

Humpbacks feed on small fish and shrimp-like animals called **krill** and **copepods**. Dense schools of fish, krill and copepods are plentiful in Alaska during the summer. Feeding whales rush through thick clouds of them, scoop up huge mouthfuls of food and water, strain the water out through their baleen, and swallow the food.

Sometimes humpbacks make a net of bubbles when they feed. They do this by diving below a school of fish and swimming in a circle while letting air out of their blowholes. As the bubbles rise toward the surface, they form a ring around the fish, almost like a curtain. The confused fish bunch together as the whale rushes up inside the curtain of bubbles with its mouth open. Humpbacks do not feed while they are in Hawai'i because there is little food for them here. Instead, they come to mate and give birth.

Mating and Birth

While in Hawai'i, humpback whales usually spend time alone, in pairs, or in small groups. They do not stay with the same companions for long, but mix and move freely from one whale (or group of whales) to the next. Adult males seem to spend most of their time looking for adult females that are ready to mate. When one is found, several males often follow her. Each male tries to chase the others away. The males bump and shove each other, and make threatening slaps on the ocean surface with their heads and tails. After the winner drives the other males away, he and the female begin to court each other by stroking, nuzzling and slapping each other with their long flippers. Sometimes a whale lies on the surface with a flipper raised in the air and slaps the water again and again.

A female that has mated will give birth when she returns to Hawai'i the following year. The **calf** can swim and breathe at birth, but it must breathe more often than adults and it can't swim as fast. Calves can only stay underwater for three to five minutes between breaths, while adults can stay underwater for ten or fifteen minutes on an average dive.

A newborn calf is about twelve feet long and weighs around one and a half tons. It grows nearly one foot per month as it nurses on its mother's milk. Mother and calf form a close bond, often touching and calling to each other as they swim. Because calves can't swim as fast as adults, the mother humpback sometimes helps her calf keep up by lifting it with her flipper or back as they swim. If a mother thinks her calf is in danger, she will move her body between the calf and the source of danger or lead her calf away toward safety.

Often, an adult male is seen swimming with a mother and calf. Sometimes this male and other adult males sing songs.

Whale Songs and Breaching

Sound travels well underwater and humpbacks have very good hearing. Unlike humans, whales can tell which direction a sound is coming from underwater. One whale can hear another whale at least two miles away. So, it is not surprising that humpback whales communicate with many different sounds. The most famous of these sounds is their long, complicated songs. A song may be six to eighteen minutes long and is made up of many repeating patterns.

Only the males sing. They all sing the same song, but the song slowly changes over the months as new patterns are added and old ones are dropped. The whales stop singing while they are in Alaska, but when they return to Hawai'i they continue the

song where they left off the year before. Males often sing while they are alone, hanging in one spot below the surface. They may sing the song over and over again. Scientists think they may sing songs to attract females.

Humpback whales are also famous for their great leaps, or **breaches**. A breaching whale thrusts itself upward until about two-thirds of its body is out of the water. Then it falls into the ocean on its back with a giant splash. No one knows why whales breach. Since whales can see well in both air and water, they may be taking a good look around. Perhaps the huge splash carries a message to other whales. Perhaps they are simply having fun or expressing joy.

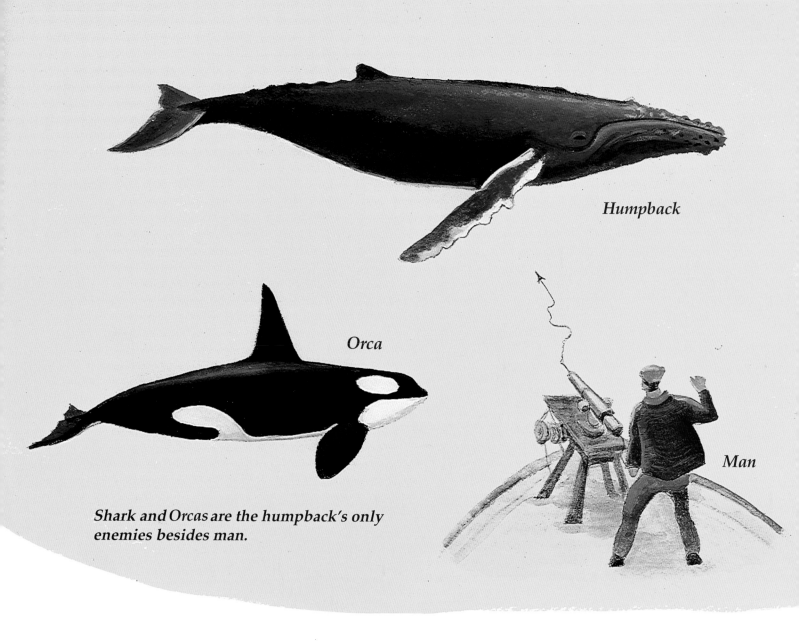

Humpback

Orca

Man

Shark and Orcas are the humpback's only enemies besides man.

Whales and Man

Men once hunted whales for their oil and fat. They killed whales in such numbers that many kinds of whales, including humpbacks, were in danger of becoming **extinct** — of disappearing from the earth forever. Today, all whales are protected by international law. Even so, some countries still hunt whales for food.

Many people who want to learn more about humpback whales come to Hawai'i because it is one of the few places where people can watch the private lives of whales up close. Whale watching has become a big business, but too many people watching the whales too closely can disturb them. People who don't mean to harm whales can cause problems in other ways too. Increased boat traffic in Hawai'i's waters and military bombing and missile practices cause noise that disturbs the sensitive hearing of dolphins and whales. These noises can interfere with communication between whales. Activities on land can also affect whales and dolphins. Chemicals from farming and other industries can enter the ocean and contaminate the food animals that whales eat.

Shark

Humpback Whale

Because humpback whales can be disturbed by boats and divers, it is against the law to come within 100 yards of a whale or to fly low overhead, buzz, or circle in a plane. These activities can frighten whales and cause them to leave the area. If whales become too disturbed by human activities, scientists fear they may decide to stop coming to Hawai'i and go elsewhere to breed and give birth.

The ancient Hawaiians did not have a name for humpback whales. In fact, there is no evidence that humpback whales were in Hawai'i before the 1700s. Many scientists think that humpbacks have only been coming to Hawai'i for the last 200 years. If so, no one knows where they went to breed before then. No one knows how long they will keep coming to Hawai'i. We do know that whales are intelligent, sensitive animals. It is important for us to give them the space and quiet they need, so that humpback whales will remain a part of Hawai'i's special marine wildlife.

Each humpback whale has marks and color patterns on the underside of its tail that are unique. Scientists use these markings, like human fingerprints, to identify each whale. By keeping track of whales, scientists gather information about where they go, what they do, and how long they live.

SPINNER DOLPHINS

The dolphins that we most often see from shore in Hawai'i are spinner dolphins. We can easily recognize them by their twirling leaps. They jump high out of the water, twisting as they rise, then fall back on their side, still spinning as they sink below the surface.

Spinner dolphins live in many parts of the Atlantic, Pacific, and Indian Oceans. Hawai'i's spinner dolphins grow slightly larger than the spinner dolphins that live in other areas and they have a beautiful three-color pattern.

Group Society

Spinner dolphins live in groups, or schools, which may include hundreds or even thousands of members. At night, a school may spread out over many miles of ocean as the dolphins hunt for food. During the day, the school breaks up into smaller schools as the dolphins move into quiet bays to rest. Resting schools usually contain no more than thirty or forty dolphins. Like humans, apes, and other mammals that live in groups, the school forms a group society. Within the school, each dolphin can find safety and friendship and meet the needs of its life.

Day Resting

Often we can see **schools** of spinner dolphins swimming along the shore in the early morning, leaping and twirling as they head toward a sheltered bay to rest for the day. As they reach their bay of rest, the leaping, noisy dolphins slow down and become quieter. They head toward a patch of white sand and move closer together until each one is swimming just beyond the reach of its neighbor's fins. As the dolphins settle down to rest, the school swims slowly, moving as one. Nearly all of the dolphins are silent. Now and then one slowly rises to the surface to take a breath of air.

Dolphins do not sleep as we do. If they did, they would stop breathing and die. Scientists believe that dolphins sleep by closing one eye while keeping the other open. This allows them to shut down, or rest, one half of their brain. The slow, silent swim of a resting dolphin is as close to "sleep" as it ever gets.

Scientists think white sand and clear water help dolphins see each other. They also expose sharks that might try to sneak up on dolphins while they are resting.
By swimming close together and moving as one, dolphins practice "safety in numbers." An attacking shark has trouble keeping track of one dolphin when all of them look the same.

Zig-Zagging

By mid-afternoon, the spinners have begun to awaken from their rest. One begins to swim faster and slaps the water with its head. Another joins in, perhaps having heard the "wake-up" splash of the first. As the dolphins become fully awake, they leap and spin, seeming ready and eager to head to sea for a night of feeding. The dolphins begin to race toward the open ocean, calling to each other and often spinning. Then the group slows down. The dolphins sense that not everyone is awake and ready yet. The group heads back to the sand patch to rest a while longer. Soon, they try another start toward the sea. And again, they quiet down and return toward land. Scientists call this back and forth movement "zig-zagging." Since the school has no leader, the dolphins seem to be testing the group—making trial runs to see if everyone is ready to go to sea. At last, all the dolphins are wide awake and the school heads out, leaping, spinning, and swimming fast toward the open sea.

Night Feeding

Members of the school spread out for the night. They join other spinner dolphins that have spent the day resting along bays around the islands. Now fully awake, they use their sonar to hunt for food and keep track of their schoolmates. Spread across miles of open ocean yet still together as a school, they hunt for fish and squid.

As dawn approaches, the dolphins head toward shore to rest. They return to the bays on a "first-come, first-serve" basis, so the members of each group in a bay may change from one day to the next.

Sonar

In the open ocean without fences or walls, a dolphin's sonar is a wonderful tool. By making a string of clicking noises and listening to the faint echoes that return, a dolphin can tell where danger is, sense its surroundings, hunt and stun its food, and keep track of its school. Scientists have discovered that a spinner dolphin using sonar can locate an object the size of an orange 370 feet away.

Sharks and other large, toothed whales may hunt spinner dolphins for food. In clear water, they have little chance of sneaking up on a dolphin that is using its sonar. Sharks can sometimes hide from sonar in cloudy water or by staying close to the bottom in shallow water.

Spinners are known to dive 200 feet deep and may dive much deeper.

Birth

Spinner dolphins and other dolphins often touch and stroke each other in ways that look to us like sex play or courtship. But these acts are more social than sexual. A female spinner dolphin is ready to mate only once or twice a year. At this time she mates with many males.

Most spinner dolphins are born in summer and fall. Like other whales and dolphins, they are born tail-first. The newborn dolphin quickly rises to the surface to take its first breath of air. Although dolphins can swim as soon as they are born, they cannot swim fast enough to keep up with the school. But by swimming close to its mother, near her forehead, a little dolphin gets pulled along by the mother's moving body in much the same way that a car gets pulled along close behind a truck that is speeding down the highway.

Scientists have discovered groups of young dolphins being looked after by older adult males. Are the old adults just "babysitting?" Are they teaching the youngsters things they need to learn? Many parts of a dolphin's life are still a mystery. Perhaps one day we will discover answers to these puzzles.

Spinning

Why do spinner dolphins spin? Is it just for fun? Spinning leaps are more common as the dolphins become more active and are most common after dark when the dolphins are spread out and using their sonar. When a dolphin is about to make a spinning leap, it first makes a short "bark," as if to announce the spin. The spin makes a swirling trail of bubbles that can be picked up by the sonar of other dolphins. These things lead scientists to think that the spin is a signal to other dolphins. Its signal may let them know the size and shape of the school at all times, so even when they are very spread out, the dolphins won't lose track of their relationship to each other.

Spinner Dolphins and Man

In the eastern Pacific Ocean, yellowfin tuna are often found in large schools below groups of spinner and spotted dolphins. Tuna fishermen use the dolphins to show them where the fish are. They surround the dolphins and tuna with giant nets. From the 1950s through the 1970s, between 300,000 and 500,000 dolphins drowned in these tuna nets each year. In the last eight years, many tuna fishermen and governments have taken steps to reduce the killing. However, the problem is still far from solved and thousands of dolphins still die each year in tuna nets. Happily, yellowfin tuna don't swim below schools of dolphins in the ocean around Hawai'i. Hawaiian spinners are safe from the nets. Still, they face other problems.

The main threat to Hawai'i's spinner dolphins probably comes from the insensitive way people live on our planet. Pollution and over-fishing are two ways that people make the ocean an unfit place for marine mammals to live. Many people are also

insensitive to the dolphins' needs for peace and privacy. A growing number of people and boats use Hawai'i's sheltered bays where spinner dolphins rest during the day. Most people don't realize that the school of spinners swimming slowly around in the bay is "sleeping," and the clean, sandy area where they swim is their "bedroom." People who learn this are usually happy to keep away and let the dolphins rest in peace. When dolphins want to play or interact with people, they will approach boats or swimmers. It is important for people who want to play with dolphins to let the dolphins make the first move. Again, don't approach dolphins—let the dolphins approach you. Even when you are hundreds of yards away from them, the dolphins know you are there. If they don't approach you, then respect their need for privacy. If people and boats continue to disturb resting spinner dolphins or dirty the ocean waters along our shores with pollution, the dolphins will be forced to leave. They will lose their quiet resting places, and we will lose the joyful sight of their gleaming, leaping shapes along our shores.

Spotted Dolphin
7'

Pygmy Killer Whale
7.5'

Melon-headed Whale
7.5'

Short-finned Pilot Whale
12'-16'

OTHER MAMMALS THAT

Many other whales and dolphins live in the tropical Pacific and are seen around Hawai'i. False killer whales and short-finned pilot whales are commonly seen offshore, but rarely swim close to land. The Pacific bottlenose dolphin is seen from December through May, often swimming with the humpback whales that come to spend the winter. Spotted dolphins, rough-toothed dolphins, pygmy killer whales, and

False Killer Whale
13'-16'

ARE HAWAI'I'S WATERS

melon-headed whales are also seen as they visit Hawai'i during their ocean travels.

We know that whales and dolphins are intelligent, curious, social animals. They can use their minds to reason, they have their different moods, and they care about each other. Yet most of the events that fill their daily lives are still unknown to us. They remain a mystery, waiting to be explored.

Rough-toothed Dolphin
7'-8'

Pacific Bottlenose Dolphin
7'-10'

THE HAWAIIAN MONK SEAL

A monk seal lies on the beach. Her long body looks like a rock worn smooth by the waves. She has been sleeping for many hours and the bright sun has made her hot. She opens her black eyes and drags herself toward the water. With her front flippers, she heaves her body forward in jerks that send rippling waves across her skin. On land she is like a slow-moving caterpillar, but in the sea she swims as lightly as a butterfly. Her streamlined body glides and twists easily, guided by her front and back flippers. Her nostrils close to keep out sea water and she holds her breath easily for ten minutes while exploring the shallow reef. She may hold her breath for twenty minutes or more while hunting for food.

Hawaiian monk seals are about seven feet long. They weigh up to 600 pounds and can live to be about thirty years old. They are different from other seals and sea lions in two important ways: they live in warm, tropical oceans and they do not group together to rest and breed.

Monk Seals Around the World

There are three species of monk seals—each named after the place where it is found. Caribbean monk seals were once killed in great numbers for food. The last Caribbean monk seal was seen in 1952. Today, not a single Caribbean monk seal remains on earth. They are extinct. Some Mediterranean monk seals still live in parts of the Mediterranean. They have been hunted and crowded out by people. Biologists are afraid that before long, the Mediterranean monk seal will also become extinct. Hawaiian monk seals, like their Caribbean and Mediterranean cousins, are few in number. Although Hawaiian monk seals are protected by law, they are in danger of disappearing forever because of human activity. With human help, however, they may remain a living part of Hawai'i's marine wildlife for years to come.

Where They Live

The Hawaiian monk seal is Hawai'i's only **endemic** marine mammal. Endemic means it lives nowhere else in the world. Most of Hawai'i's monk seals live among the Northwestern Hawaiian Islands. Few people live on these islands, and the plentiful beaches and flat rock shorelines of some islands make good places for the monk seals to rest and give birth to their young. Monk seals rarely move away from the island where they were born, although some move to other islands within the Hawaiian chain. In recent years, a few monk seals have made the main islands their homes.

These seals were probably called "monk" seals because they like to live alone. Monk seals don't like to lie next to each other, but they do like to lie next to other objects, such as fishing floats, rocks, or even sea turtles.

The monk seal's Hawaiian name, 'ilio-holo-i-ka-uaua, means "the dog that runs in the tough elements." It is a good name for this dog-faced mammal that can swim through rough waves, but it is not a very old name. If there was an ancient Hawaiian name, it has been lost. Perhaps the ancient Hawaiians had no name for the monk seal because it rarely visited the islands where people lived, and it was not used by the Hawaiians as an important food.

What They Eat

Monk seals eat many kinds of marine animals. They usually hunt at night, catching reef fish, moray eels, octopus, sea cucumbers, and lobsters on the shallow reefs around their home island. They also spend much time at sea and can dive as deep as 500 feet.

Mating

Most seals and sea lions gather on land in large groups, or harems, during the breeding season. Each group is made up of many females and one male. The male fights off other males who want to mate with the females in his group. This protects the females from the unwelcome attention of too many males, and it allows the male to mate with each member of his group. Monk seals don't gather in these harems. They live alone and mate in the water instead of on land. When an adult female is ready to mate, any male may try to mate with her. This is causing a problem in some areas where the numbers of males and females are out of balance. On most of the Northwestern Hawaiian Islands, there are about equal numbers of males and females. But on two of these islands there are many more males than females. Sometimes several males try to mate with a female at once. She can become injured and exhausted, and sometimes dies. Each time this happens, there are fewer females and the problem gets worse. Biologists are working to solve this problem by bringing the number of males and females back into balance.

A pup nurses from four nipples on its mother's belly.

Birth

One year after mating, the female comes ashore to give birth. Although females sometimes give birth to a new **pup** each year, they usually have one pup every two years. The best shorelines for giving birth are quiet beaches where the water is shallow and sheltered. Shallow water protects the mother and pup from tiger sharks, a main enemy. Sheltered water protects the pup from being washed out to sea by large waves.

Pups are usually born between February and August, with most pups being born in May. A newborn monk seal pup is about three feet long and is covered with black, fuzzy fur. Like most newborn mammals, the pup does little for the first few days besides sleep and drink milk.

Mother and pup stay close together and communicate often with barks and groans. After a few days, the mother takes her pup for short trips into shallow water to cool off from the baking sun. She is a patient parent and lies quietly while her playful pup chews on her flippers and wiggles its sandy body across her head.

The mother stays on the beach with her pup for about six weeks. She doesn't eat during this time but instead lives off the layer of **blubber**, or fat, under her skin. As the pup grows plump and round on her rich milk, she becomes thin.

Slowly the pup grows stronger and its black fur is replaced by a coat of silver-gray fur on the back and creamy white fur on the belly. As the fur gets older, it will slowly turn brown on top and yellow on the belly. Each year, the seal will **molt** and the old hairs will fall out. As the old hairs fall off along with the top layer of skin, they expose a new coat of silver-gray fur growing underneath.

At the end of six weeks, the mother is very hungry. It is time for her to leave the pup and feed herself. She returns to the sea, leaving the pup on its own. The pup has nobody to teach it how to hunt or show it what to eat. Hopefully, the pup is as fat as a balloon when the mother leaves. It will need to live off this body fat for about six months while it learns how to feed itself. Sometimes two pups on the same beach will switch mothers by mistake. (The mother seals don't seem to recognize one pup from another.) If an older pup and a younger pup switch mothers, the older pup will get to nurse for longer than usual. But the younger pup may not get to nurse as long as it needs to. If a nursing pup doesn't grow fat enough, it will starve before it learns to feed itself.

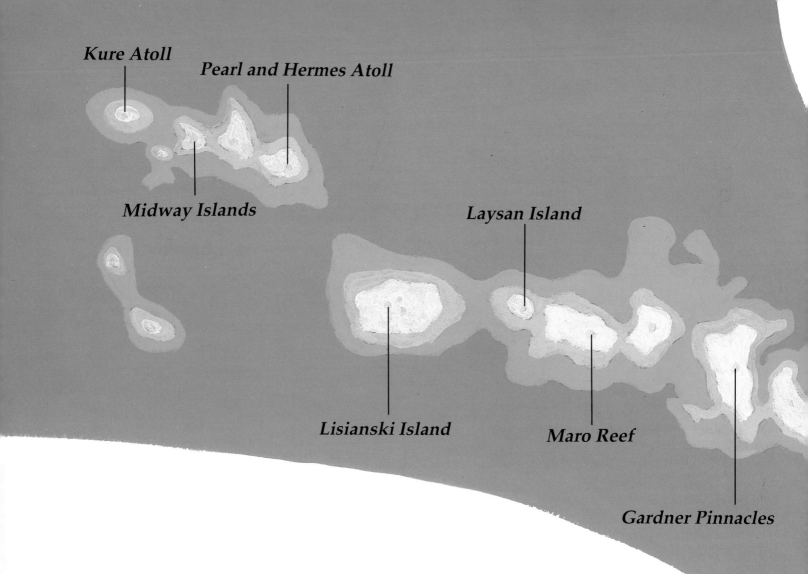

Kure Atoll

Pearl and Hermes Atoll

Midway Islands

Laysan Island

Lisianski Island

Maro Reef

Gardner Pinnacles

Monk Seals and Man

Monk seals are shy, private animals that are easily disturbed by people. Although resting seals don't often run from people, this doesn't mean they are not disturbed. Monk seals are often very tired when they come ashore to rest. They may be sleeping too soundly to know that people are on the beach. But once awake, a disturbed seal may leave the beach before it is fully rested. Just the presence of people on a beach walking, playing, or taking pictures can be enough to make a monk seal leave its favorite beach. This means more than just lack of sleep for the seal. Getting enough rest can mean the difference between life and death.

Mother monk seals with pups are easily upset by people. They sometimes leave the beach before the pup is ready to be on its own, causing the pup to starve. Dogs that run loose on the beach can also frighten and hurt monk seals. As beaches become more crowded with people, there is less room for monk seals. As the ocean becomes more full of boats and swimmers, there is less room for monk seals to swim and hunt for food.

In 1909, the Hawaiian Islands National Wildlife Refuge was created to protect Hawaiian wildlife, including monk seals. Here, monk seals can find the food and space they need in order to live. People are not allowed to visit these islands without special permission. Unfortunately, the rubbish that is thrown overboard by careless people on boats and ships reaches every island. Curious monk seals sometimes get stuck in plastic straps and old fish nets that people have thrown overboard. Fish hooks can cut them and get stuck in their mouths, causing infection.

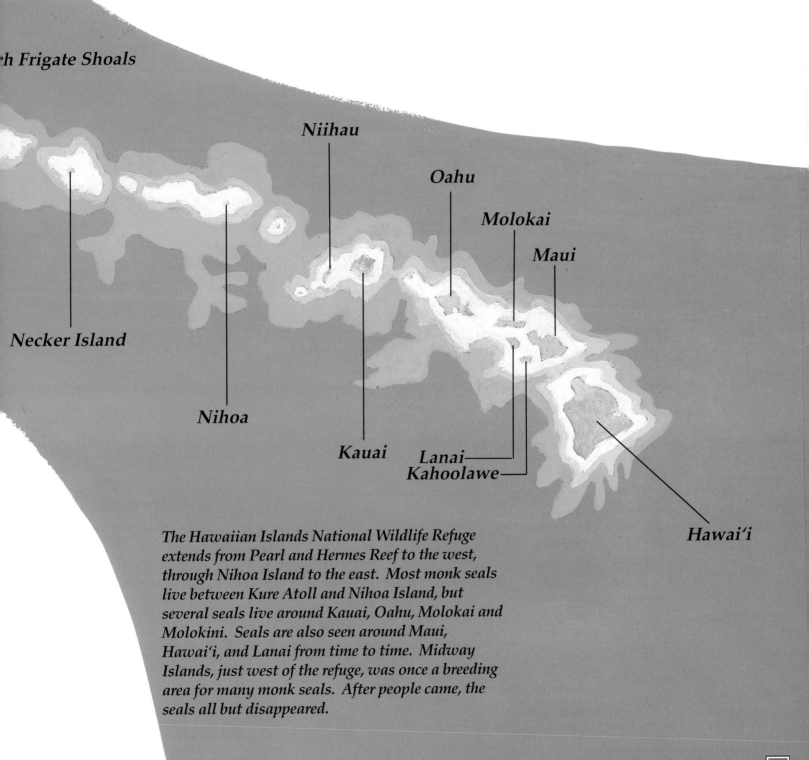

h Frigate Shoals

Niihau

Oahu

Molokai

Maui

Necker Island

Nihoa

Kauai

Lanai
Kahoolawe

Hawai'i

The Hawaiian Islands National Wildlife Refuge extends from Pearl and Hermes Reef to the west, through Nihoa Island to the east. Most monk seals live between Kure Atoll and Nihoa Island, but several seals live around Kauai, Oahu, Molokai and Molokini. Seals are also seen around Maui, Hawai'i, and Lanai from time to time. Midway Islands, just west of the refuge, was once a breeding area for many monk seals. After people came, the seals all but disappeared.

The Future

Like humpback whales, monk seals are an endangered species—in danger of becoming extinct—and are protected by law. Although it is against the law to catch, harm, kill or disturb monk seals, the real danger does not come from people who want to hurt the seals. It comes from people who want to get close to them out of curiosity. Once people learn that monk seals need space and privacy, they are usually glad to watch the seals from a distance.

Every year, some visitors find a monk seal lying on the beach. They think the seal must be sick or dying and try to help it by pushing or chasing it back to the water. They do not understand that the monk seal is sleeping and must be left alone. By sending the sleeping seal back to sea, they are hurting it instead of helping it.

Biologists are studying Hawaiian monk seals and helping them survive. And people like you and I are helping, too. In recent years, two monk seal pups were born on Oʻahu and Kauaʻi. On each island, residents came together and formed a group of "babysitters" for the mother and pup. Day and night for six weeks, babysitters took turns guarding the seals by keeping people and dogs from getting too close. Their efforts worked. Both monk seal pups grew fat and healthy on their mothers' milk, and are living in Hawaiʻi's waters today.

MONK SEALS—DO'S AND DON'TS

1. DO stay at least 100 feet away from a seal on the beach.

2. If you must pass a seal on the beach, DO so quietly and DO try to keep the seal from seeing you.

3. DON'T approach a seal either on land or in water. A monk seal may swim over to look at you or your boat, but DON'T follow or chase it.

4. If you see a monk seal that is hurt or if you see someone bothering a seal, DO call the National Marine Fisheries Service, or the number below and report it right away.

The Conservation Hotline is an emergency environmental number that works throughout the state. Dial "0" and ask the operator to connect you with "Enterprise 5469."

GLOSSARY

baleen - the horny material that forms fringed plates that hang from the upper jaw of baleen whales. It is used to strain bits of food from sea water. Another name for baleen is whalebone.

blowhole - an opening used for breathing, located at the top of the head of dolphins and whales. The pressure of water keeps the blowhole closed when the dolphin or whale is underwater. Muscles open the blowhole when the animal needs to breathe.

blubber - the thick layer of fat beneath the skin of many marine mammals.

calf, calves - the young of certain animals including whales and cows.

echolocation - a sensing system using sound. By producing sounds and receiving their echoes, an animal such as a dolphin can learn information about the world, such as the direction and distance of objects underwater.

endemic - an animal or plant that occurs only in a certain region.

endangered species - a kind of plant or animal that is faced with the danger of becoming extinct.

extinct - no longer existing on earth.

magnetite - a mineral which comes from iron.

mammal - animals which breathe air, have hair, and are able to maintain a warm body temperature even when the surroundings are cold. Female mammals can produce milk to feed their young.

migration - movement from one region to another. Many animals including birds, fish and whales, migrate each year, back and forth, between the same places.

molt - to shed all or part of an outer covering from time to time. This outer covering, such as hair, skin, or feathers, is then replaced by new growth.

nurse - to drink milk from the mother.

pup - the young of certain animals including seals and dogs.

school - a group of certain animals including dolphins and fish.

society - a group of people or animals who live and interact together.

sonar - see echolocation.

I N D E X

Kure Atoll

Midway Islands

Pearl and Hermes Atoll

Lisianski Island

Laysan Island

Maro Reef

Gardner Pinnacles

PACIFIC